To Ian, Jess, Jude and the city

First published in the United States in 2002
by Chronicle Books LLC.

Copyright © 2002 by Adria Meserve.
Originally published in the U. K. in 2002
by Bodley Head Children's Books
a division of Random House U. K.
All rights reserved.

North American text design by Sara Gillingham.
Typeset in Garbage.
The illustrations in this book were
rendered in gouache and collage.
Manufactured in Singapore.

Library of Congress Cataloging-in-Publication
Data available.

Distributed in Canada by Raincoast Books
9050 Shaughnessy Street
Vancouver, British Columbia V6P 6E5

10 9 8 7 6 5 4 3 2 1

Chronicle Books LLC
85 Second Street
San Francisco, California 94105

www.chroniclekids.com

Smog
the
City Dog

by Adria Meserve

chronicle books·san francisco

Smog the city dog was hungry.
All the trash cans on his street were empty,
and the sidewalks were swept clean.

"I've got to find some food!" Smog said.

His tummy rumbled louder than a diesel truck.

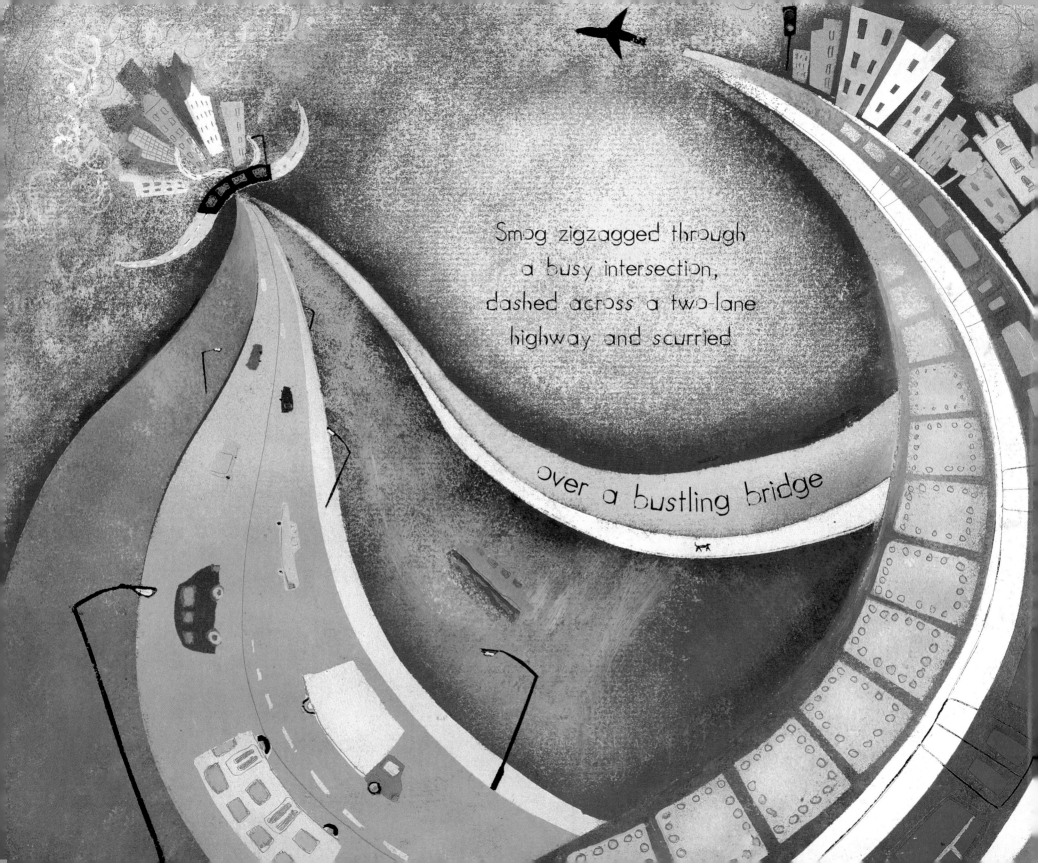

Smog zigzagged through
a busy intersection,
dashed across a two-lane
highway and scurried

over a bustling bridge

to a quiet canal.

If only he could find a snack!
He sniffed the air.

Could it be?

. . . Dinner!

Smog
snatched
the bag
of food and
ran.

"Sausages," Smog said and smiled, slowing down to a casual trot.

"Now all I need is a quiet place to eat."

But Smog wasn't the only one who was hungry.

Squirrel smelled something tasty.

Cat's nose perked up.

Fox was hot on his heels.

"Buzz off!"

growled Smog, picking up the pace.

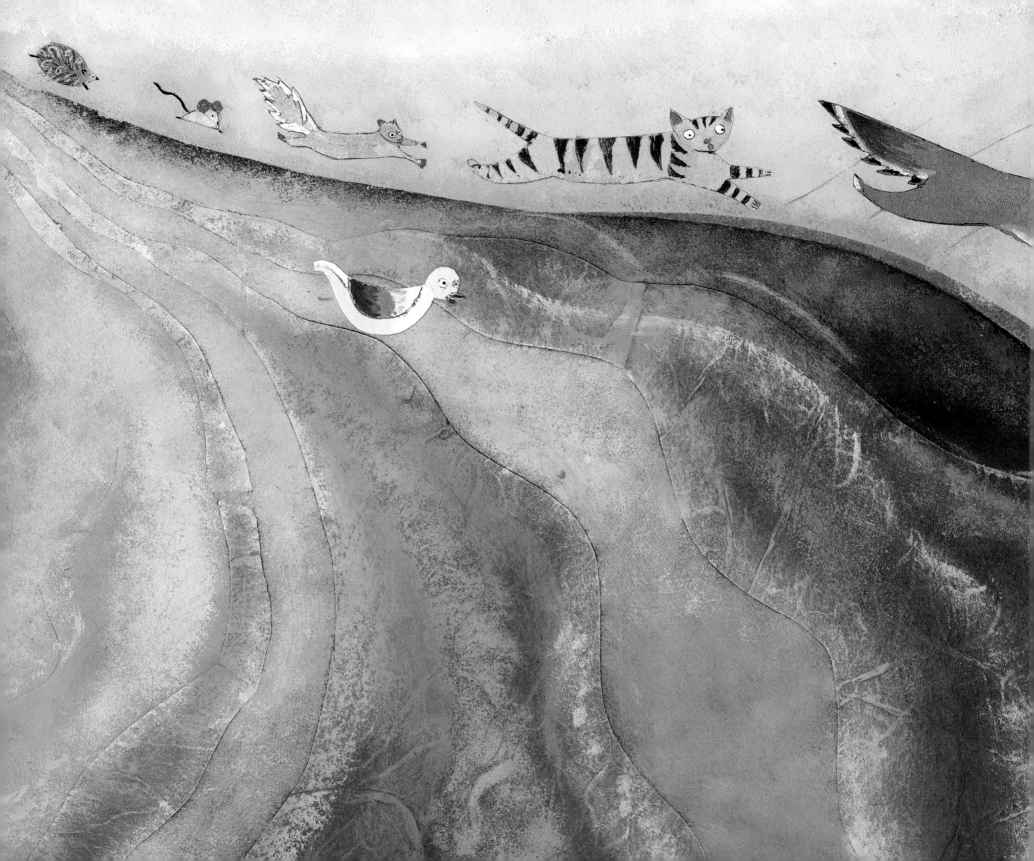

"WOOF!"

he barked at the other dog.

SPLASH!

went the bag.

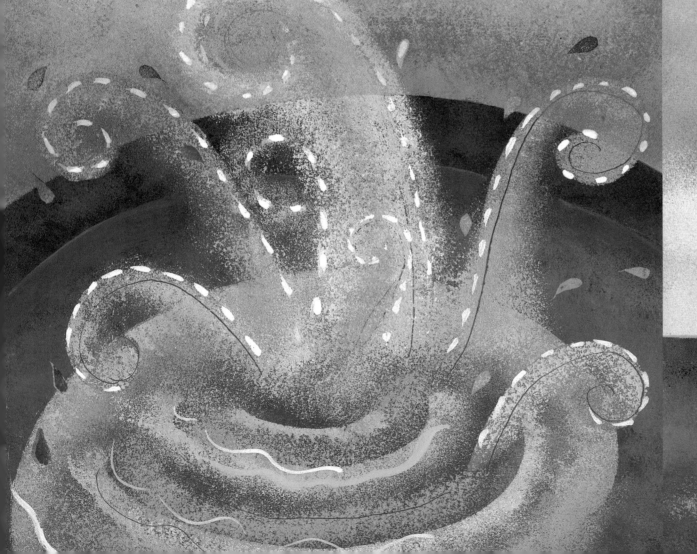

GLUG,
GLUG,
GLUG.

Everyone watched it sink.

"Quack!" said the ducks, diving down for the bag. "It's too heavy for us!"

"I'm strong," boasted Fox. "Let me try."
But the water was too deep.

"To the bridge!" squeaked Mouse. "I've got a plan!"

"Heave ho!" barked Smog.

"You can do it!" shouted Porcupine.

"Just a few more feet," the ducks said, "and it's time for…."

"...our dinner!" said Smog.
"A tummy full of food and a park full of friends.
What more could any city dog want?"